The Extraordinary Dreidel

A Hanukkah Story from Israel

Written by Devorah Omer

Illustrated by Aviel Basil

Translated by Shira Atik

Green
Bean
Books

On Hanukkah, Uncle Haim the carpenter made Gil and Nurit a wooden dreidel. This was no ordinary dreidel. It was as big as a soccer ball!

And it had a hidden compartment! If you pressed down the letter *nun* — which stands for *nes* (miracle) and also for *nistar* (hidden) — the cover popped open! Behind it, there was a secret hiding place.

"What should we hide inside?" Ima asked.
"All my prize certificates!" Abba replied.
"How about my stamp collection?" Gil asked.
"No," Nurit said. "My doll needs a closet for her clothes!"

They couldn't decide. Everyone had an idea — everyone except Mitzi the cat. She was tired, so she just curled up on the sofa to rest.

The next morning, Gil said, "I have an idea! I know how to figure out what to put inside the dreidel. I'll take it to my school Hanukkah party, and whoever has the best idea wins a prize!"

"I bet your friends will have some great ideas!" Nurit added.

Gil couldn't wait for the Hanukkah party.
But first he had to go to school.
"I have a surprise," Gil whispered to his teacher
and friends, "but I'm not going to show it to you now.
You'll see at the party."
Everyone was curious, but Gil wouldn't say another word.

That afternoon, when he came home from school, Gil looked for the dreidel to get ready for the party . . . but it was nowhere to be found! "Ima, Abba, where's my dreidel? Can you help me find it?" he asked.

Ima looked, Abba looked, Nurit and Gil looked — but they found nothing. The dreidel had disappeared!

"Where could it be?" Gil asked, with tears in his eyes.
"I can't go to the party without it. I'll let everyone down!"
"Go anyway," Abba suggested. "I'm sure we'll find the dreidel
while you're there, and we can bring it to you."

Gil nodded. He went to the closet to get his jacket, and when he opened the door, he was surprised to hear a soft *meow* coming from behind the coats.

Gil pushed them aside only
to discover something
extraordinary . . .

At the back of the closet was the dreidel! It was open, and inside were four tiny kittens. Next to them lay Mitzi, looking proud.

That evening, Gil didn't take the dreidel to the party. He didn't want to disturb the kittens, and so he left them snuggled up inside.

When he told his classmates about the dreidel and the kittens, no one could believe it. It was a true Hanukkah miracle! They wanted to see for themselves.

Finally, they all knew what belonged in the dreidel. Everyone agreed it was Nun, Gimmel, Hay and Peh — four Hanukkah kittens named for the four dreidel letters.

Green
Bean
Books

First published in the UK in 2023 by Green Bean Books
c/o Pen & Sword Books Ltd
47 Church Street, Barnsley, South Yorkshire, S70 2AS
www.greenbeanbooks.com
Text copyright © Devorah Omer, 2022
Illustrations copyright © Aviel Basil, 2021
English edition © Green Bean Books, 2023
First published in Israel by Modan Publishing in 2021 as the result of the initiative
of Keren Grinspoon's Sifriyat Pijama program in Israel.
Shira Atik English-language translation has been used with the permission of Sifriyat Pijama
Green Bean Books edition: 978-17843-8937-6
Harold Grinspoon Foundation edition ISBN 978-17843-8941-3

Designed by Ian Hughes
Edited by Malu Rocha and Rachael Stein
Production by Hugh Allan

Printed in China by Leo Paper Products Ltd
1123/B2468/A5

FSC
www.fsc.org
MIX
Paper | Supporting
responsible forestry
FSC® C020056